Galapagos Flamingo

Warbler

Marine Iguana

Galapagos
Penguin

Sally
Lightfoot
Crab

Lava Lizard

Galapagos
Tortoise

Benjamin's Blue Feet

Sue Macartney

pajamapress

First published in Canada and the United States in 2020

The publisher gratefully acknowledges the support of the Canada Council for the Arts and the Ontario Arts Council for its publishing program. We acknowledge the financial support of the Government of Canada through the Canada Book Fund (CBF) for our publishing activities.

Library and Archives Canada Cataloguing in Publication

Title: Benjamin's blue feet / Sue Macartney.
Names: Macartney, Sue, 1959- author, illustrator.
identifiers: Canadiana 20200165968 | iSBN 9781772781113 (softcover)
Classification: LCC PS8625.A232 B46 2020 | DDC jC813/.6—dc23

Publisher Cataloging-in-Publication Data (U.S.)

Names: Macartney, Sue, author, illustrator.
Title: Benjamin's Blue Feet / Sue Macartney.
Description: Toronto, Ontario Canada : Pajama Press, 2020. | Summary: "A young blue-footed booby named Benjamin has a knack for finding "treasure" (human discards). When his discovery of a mirror causes him to become insecure about his body, Benjamin uses his collection to change his features. But his changes make it impossible to swim and fish and fly, and Benjamin realizes he's exactly the way he's meant to be" -- Provided by publisher.
identifiers: iSBN 978-1-77278-111-3 (hardcover)
Subjects: LCSH: Blue-footed booby — Juvenile fiction. | individual differences — Juvenile fiction. | Body image — Juvenile fiction. | BiSAC: JUVENiLE FiCTiON / Animals / Birds. | JUVENiLE FiCTiON / Social Themes / Self-Esteem & Self-Reliance.
Classification: LCC PZ7.1M333Ben |DDC [E] — dc23

Original art created with pen and ink and digital media
Cover and book design—Rebecca Bender

Manufactured in China by WKT Company

Pajama Press inc.
181 Carlaw Ave. Suite 251 Toronto, Ontario Canada, M4M 2S1

Distributed in Canada by UTP Distribution
5201 Dufferin Street Toronto, Ontario Canada, M3H 5T8

Distributed in the U.S. by ingram Publisher Services
1 ingram Blvd. La Vergne, TN 37086, USA

For my children
Andrew and Emma

For a downloadable glossary of facts
about Galapagos wildlife, visit

pajamapress.ca/resource/benjamins_blue_feet_extra_content

Benjamin is a little booby.
A little **blue-footed booby.**
A little treasure-hunting blue-footed booby.

The best little treasure-hunting
blue-footed booby on the island!

Yesterday he found a long, red something.
A...**string-stretch-it?**

The day before he found a round something.
A...hmmm...a...hole-thing-um?
What will he find at the beach today?

"Look!" shouts Benjamin. "A shiny something.
A twinkly something. A...hmmm...a...
twink-um-doodle!"

Hello?

He circles slowly around to the twinkliest side.
"Why, that's me!" Benjamin gasps.
"This is the best treasure—EVER."

He flaps and **honk -honk HONKS!**

"Back to my hiding place!"

Excited, Benjamin peers at himself.

He stares at his beak.

It's straight.
And very long—
not like Warbler's
tiny beak.

Benjamin stares at his wings.

They are wide and long and bristly—not like
Penguin's sleek and narrow wings that hug his body.

Benjamin stares at his feet.

They are floppy...and BLUE—not like Iguana's clawed toes that cling to the rocks.

Benjamin is miserable.

He doesn't want that twink-um-doodle anymore!
"I'll bury it, BURY IT!" he cries.

Suddenly, Benjamin has an idea.
He searches through his treasures.

"What if I take my
string-stretch-its?
Then my feet won't look so blue."

"I'll just squeeze into my
hole-thing-um.
Then my wings won't stick out."

"This **old plunk-it** is
perfect to shorten my beak!"

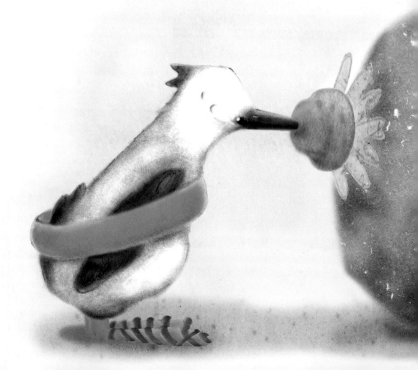

Benjamin holds his breath and **wobble-waddles** to the beach.

The iguanas bob-bob their heads in surprise.

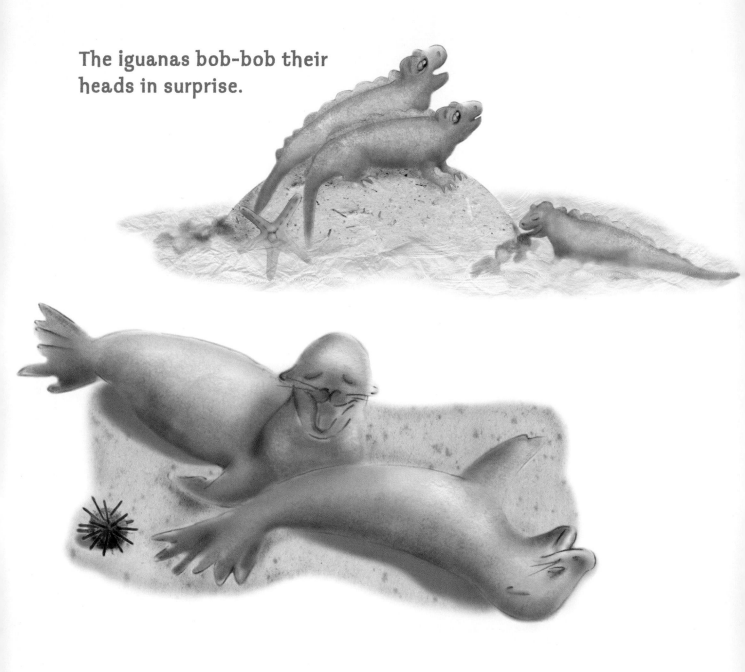

The sea lions rock to and fro with laughter.

A flock of finches erupts
in a twittering kerfuffle.

Benjamin ignores them and totters on.

He launches himself and lands—
beak-first in the waves!

"Oh no! I can't swim
without my big feet."
He
kick-flips,
    flap-slaps,

until the
string-stretch-its
SNAP off.

A shimmering school of fish flashes by.
Benjamin jabs at them, but his beak bop-bops BACK!
"Oh no! I can't fish without my beak."

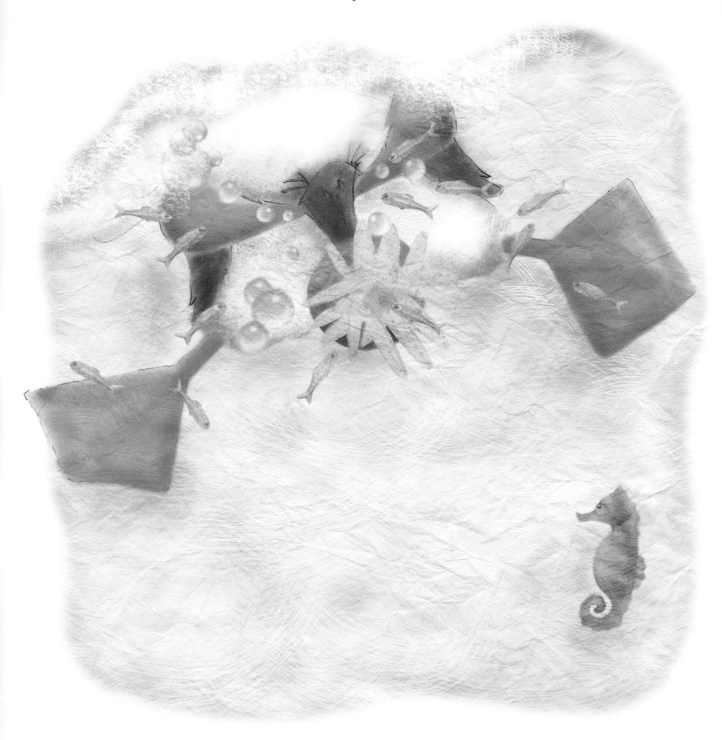

He
wriggle-wiggles,
joggle-jiggles

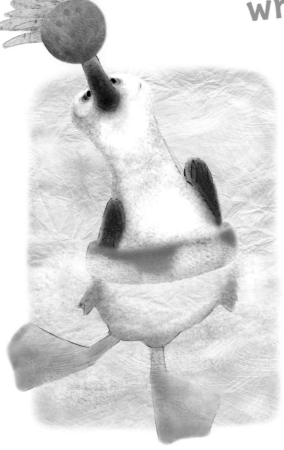

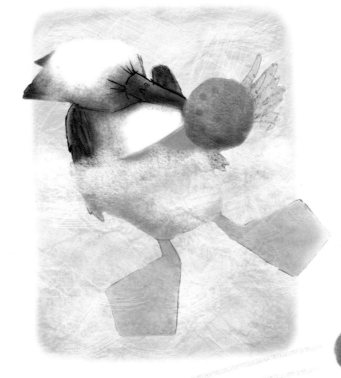

until that **old plunk-it**
SHOOTS off.

Just then, a flock of blue-footed boobies
soars into the sky.

It's fishing time!
Benjamin tries to flap his wings...
but they're stuck!

"Oh no!
I can't fly without
my wings."

Benjamin
churn-turns,
worm-squirms,

until the
hole-thing-um POPS off.

Benjamin paddles in happy circles.
"I am a **blue-footed booby**,

so of course my feet are **BLUE!**
Perfect for paddling."

"Of course my beak is long and pointy.
Superb for catching fish."

"And how could I fly without my wide wings?"

Benjamin stretches his wings and feels a delightful, tingly sensation, right down to the ends of his big, blue feet.

Wait for MEEE

Then Benjamin soars high into the sky to join the other boobies.

A Note about Trash in the Ocean

Benjamin, like many blue-footed boobies, lives in the Galapagos Islands, which are famous for their many unique creatures. Some, like the Galapagos Marine Iguana, live nowhere else in the world. This means it's especially important to protect them.

Benjamin's story is about body image, but it's also about a wild, wonderful place where few humans visit—but the beaches are still full of trash. Waste from all over the world finds its way into the ocean, and it causes major problems for sea life and the creatures who live along shorelines.

it's important for us all to help reduce waste and to make sure that what we do throw away is processed properly. Working together, we can keep beaches beautiful and protect our ocean wildlife.